*For Nate*

*With very special thanks to Mum, Dad, Rosy and Finlay, Oats and the Abbots Lodge cat gang*

*— J.K.R.*

Clarion Books
3 Park Avenue
New York, New York 10016

Clarion Books is an imprint of Houghton Mifflin Harcourt Publishing Company.

hmhbooks.com

The text was set in Paper Cuts Regular.
Book design by Elliot Kreloff

Library of Congress Cataloging-in-Publication Data
Names: Rayner, Jacqueline K., author, illustrator.
Title: Hats are not for cats! / Jacqueline K. Rayner.
Description: Boston ; New York : Clarion Books, Houghton Mifflin Harcourt, 2019. |
Summary: A patronizing, plaid-hat-wearing dog informs a cat that hats are only for dogs but the cat,
joined by others, dons a wide assortment of hats proving, at last, that hats are for everyone.
Identifiers: LCCN 2018051215 (print) | LCCN 2018055095 (ebook) | ISBN
9780358063605 | ISBN 9781328967190 (hardback) | ISBN 9780358063605 (e-book)
Subjects: | CYAC: Stories in rhyme. | Cats--Fiction. | Dogs--Fiction. |
Hats--Fiction. | Humorous stories. | BISAC: JUVENILE FICTION / Animals /
Cats. | JUVENILE FICTION / Animals / Dogs. | JUVENILE FICTION / Humorous Stories.
Classification: LCC PZ8.3.R23328 (ebook) | LCC PZ8.3.R23328 Hat 2019 (print) | DDC [E]--dc23
LC record available at https://lccn.loc.gov/2018051215

Manufactured in Malaysia
TWP 10 9 8 7 6 5 4 3 2
4500771618

# HATs ARE NOT FOR CATs!

JACQUELINE K. RAYNER

**Clarion Books**

HOUGHTON MIFFLIN HARCOURT

Boston    New York

Excuse me, cat.
I see you're wearing a hat,
but hats . . .

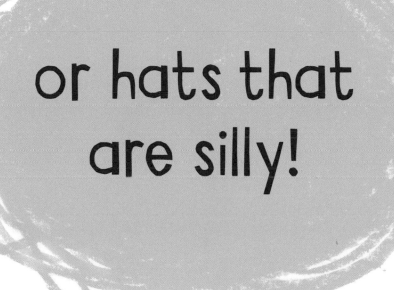

or hats that
are silly!

HATS
N
FOR

Hats....